I0456633

The Moss Wall

Liam Mac an Ghoill

ISBN: 0956907113
ISBN13: 978-0956907110

ALSO BY LIAM MAC AN GHOILL

The Chronicles of Tiny Tim
Among The Shadows Of Men
Face2Face

CONTENTS

A Novella

1

A CANE FOR EVERY PAIN

If I was to add one word that would shiver wildly from that cold musty December breath, the word pain in all essence would be distinct in its meaning. Pain from the synchronized Christmas decorations streaming above my ten-year-old head. Pain from the dripping lemonade flowing in grief from the age-stained classroom desk, and pain from the polished bamboo cane screaming down from authority to seek vengeance from the hands of the innocence. Through the frosted optical panes of observance, small familiar faces zoom in on my position beside the blackboard; a few sympathetic portraits meaningful in their intentions were blotched out by the glare of marble leers. Leers that only strengthened my resolve to depart from my childhood for a few unruly minutes and stand within the shadows of men.

Christmas party 1974 by no means give alms to the festive moment, for whenever pain in its broad dark merciless form arrives to swallow compassion, festive amnesty is smothered among the scraps of silent wishes. On the grey classroom floor I am forced to dry the stray contents of my paper cup with the sleeve of my brown worn pullover, stalling only to allow the cold moisture to salve my burning hands. Two large laced boots stamped their presence, asserting their watch for the completion of my task.

'McKenna! Sloppiness and smearing of school property will not be tolerated', roared the headmaster. I stole a glance from my indignant state of inhumanity and whispered that accident was a useful word to describe what had happened.

'Accident is also a word to describe what you are boy, something that was unintentional and should never have been allowed to happen', breathed the headmaster.

The long drowning seconds that followed came to a murdering end by three thumping consecutive knocks straining the timber of the yellow classroom door.

In the air of his entrance the school inspector's wraith freed me from my sin; allowing me to mould in equal unison with my fellow youngsters, together forging the morning's status to be in keeping with the moment.

'Good morning Mr. Evans', we sang.

'Good morning children, you may be seated', he replied in a voice that sang to the tune of a rasping file.

I regained my seat and watched the headmaster done his formal mask while reaching for the roll book bearing the heavy chains of my absence. The inspector focused his eyes, going down each page in search of black wool among the lambs. My stare returns to the headmaster, his excitement moves within his lichen circle, flowing in frenzied glee to arrive at the sacrificial ritual to slay the object of his discontent. A consoling breeze enters through the open window to sooth my rosy fear with winter hush. Within the cavern of my skull my brain begs to hear the midday toll, closing the pages of torment to depart to the hour of food. I hear my name called once again; I am alone.

'McKenna! McKenna!' roared the inspector, 'I would like a word, could you please follow me to the staff room'.

From the chair in my condemned cell I arise, from the distance a funeral bell chimes ten notes; a note for every year of my heart-rending miserable existence.

Behind the hangman I march slowly along the stretch of disinfected corridor, a passage that echoed the pleading voice of my mother.

'For God's sake son will you go to school, they'll put you into a reform school', the tone in her voice unbeknown to the nettles that clung to my flesh, within the growth of humiliation, suffering and cruelty where I was sent to learn.

I hear the headmaster's voice punching my bag of thoughts; (An accident should not be allowed to happen, you must not happen). As the noose hovers above my head, I offer myself to the acceptance of my fate.

'Close the door behind you young fella', said Mr. Evans, refusing to take leave of his rasping voice.

I obeyed.

'Sit down', he said.

As I positioned my backside on the solid wooden

chair he spoke again.

'Well son, one hundred days off school this year is totally unacceptable, what excuse have you conjured up for me this time?' he asked.

I had prepared myself for this very moment, a defence strategy had been fashioned with precise detail, each line carefully designed to throw light into the darkness of my predicament. In the peaceful hours prior to my slumber in consultation with my brother John, I had designed the perfect speech. An excuse that would shake the very foundations of disbelief; a lie that would crumble the solid stone pillars of honesty.

'I was sick', I blurted out, smothering the carefully prepared excuse under the pillow of confusion.

'Are you sure you didn't die?' asked Mr. Evans

'No', I replied.

'Are you going to die?' asked Mr. Evans

'No', I sniffed once again.

'Thank goodness for that', said Mr. Evans, 'taking one hundred days off school does warrant a very serious illness and in your case you look as healthy as a greyhound'.

I sat in silence, not daring to challenge his assessment of the present situation.

'Is something bothering you at school son?' he asked.

'Yes', I cried inwardly, 'free me from this pulsating cage of wretchedness', at this moment I redirected the coming convoy of tears and stuttered 'no', driving out the dozers of emotion that threatened to tumble my outer defence.

'Well wee man', replied the inspector, 'it has now reached a serious situation, if there is not a vast improvement in the next term I am afraid your parents will be issued with a summons to appear in court and you will go to a reform school'.

It was then that I could feel the trap door prepare to open below my feet. The four walls pulsated in rhythm with my heart to pound the room with my unbearable presence, and the grey blanket of mist that had once become a symbol of wonder creeping across the Glen Shane mountains, had now arrived to pay host to my future vision. I studied the deep lines on Mr. Evan's face, the crevices that contained the secrets of his life. His deep brown sober eyes wore the curtains of his responsibility. His head had now become a barren pasture, laid bare by the drought of age. From the window of my observation I could hear his voice yet again calling my attention.

'Young fella', he said, 'next term you're going to have to improve even if you die; school may not be the most exciting place to be, but it is compulsory and as long as I am here to enforce it, you will abide by these rules'.

I did not speak, resolving only to challenge his deep prolonged stare and search for one small fragment of pretence. The dinner bell rang aloud to triple with the shredded nerves and hunger that yelled from the Well of my stomach. He beckoned for me to go and from the fixed noose my soul departed; to flow in swing with the momentary throngs of famine victims to the glory of the dinner hall.

I dare not stand at the head of the table in search of server's perks, I positioned myself in common form at the table's side, muttered grace and gratefully collected my accepted meagre serving of one potato, one sausage and ten red beans. The customary ration of taunts and insults arranged itself over my plate like vultures seeking their pound of raw flesh. The introduction of this adversity was fashioned in the form of collected swabs of saliva taking refuge upon my begrudging portion of nourishment. As a direct result, no other action lesser than to inflict pain on the culprits could be considered and amidst the broken plates, scattered food and tumbled chairs, I am forcibly removed by the hair by a much superior force of strength, age and baldness. I yet again arrive in the classroom of pain and without reservation claim responsibility for the death of two healthy bamboo canes. In the silence of the conclusion of my chastisement, I am alone in the schoolyard. I give praise to the clotted curdled sleet and snow camouflaging my tired face. In the depth of my resilience I cloak my pride with weakness, unable to behold the shadows of men. I exist only for the last moments of term.

I now rest upon nature's high carpet of emerald grass, speckled by yellow Ben weeds and docken leaves; my schoolbag protects me from the soggy December ground. At the field's edge the holly tree stands in solitary fame, ruby dotted on virgin ground, attentively awaiting the caress of human touch. I reach out gently removing the rich festive branches one by one and embrace their jagged thorns with mild irritation. Tying the branches carefully together with a length of discarded bailer twine I take possession of my schoolbag and proceed to make my way home. The trail leads me through customary places, past cottages and two storey houses, under fir trees and to the entrance of Peter's farmyard where dragon geese await the arrival of inferior footsteps. I wrap the strap of my tan leather schoolbag around my right arm and prepare to indulge it in a far greater use than it was foremost intended. From the secluded corner of the old pebble dashed farmhouse the fowl ambush commenced, only to be diluted among the mass of flying leather and gliding feathers, swiftly handing in their resignation once again and retreating back to their affronted aviary habitat. With my fowl enemies quickly and easily defeated, I afforded myself a quick introduction to the corrugated metal roof of Peter's house. This was instigated in the form of a well in proportion stone, that was delivered with enough force required to make the journey home in one eighth of the expectant time. This vast reduction in length was brought to me courtesy of Peter's infuriating folded down Wellington boot wraith pursuing me with vengeful and unhealthy intentions. It was commonly in Peter's best interests to fall back on his hot pursuit at the approach to the back garden of my place of residence. Not for the fear of paternal scrutiny, but the likelihood of treading on canine ground. This was quickly accepted by the excited bark of a flea-riddled expression of man's best friend, slapping its odour-soaked tongue kindly over my face; disgustingly laying claim to my friendship. In all honesty, Jip the quad-legged mutt was indeed worthy of that reward. An intelligent creature well in excess of its cold-blooded expectancy. An obedient humble animal, never backward when it came to displaying its molars in your defence during any argument.

As I made my way to the back door leading to the

small but cosy scullery, I could smell the strong domestic aroma of freshly baked soda bread; tenderly signalling to the homeward bound. The creak of the green tired panelled door announced my entrance, allowing me to take refuge within a mixture of deep human embrace and the white flour that powdered my mother's blue checked apron. I live for the coming home from school, to stand at the corner of my maternal street and consume the clean pure drop of liquid normality. Within my mother's dome the smooth warm air of security rises to surround the nurtured bubble that I am safe within. In an entry in the logbook of life I am now a breathing fort, a sheath of corn surrounded by the mist of invisibility. I am a torch light wagging through the blackness of harm, brighter than the sun. Beside my tea, rhubarb and scone, as the clock taps lazily by, I am immune from all disease. Go away headmaster, go away school inspector, Inspector! The word exploded into a million different fragments of shattered hopes, the scone now became lodged somewhere between my tongue and the dark cavity of my despair. Words cold in their sounds jetted through the stream of my memory of some hours earlier; reform school, summons, execution, now became solid in their ugliness. My thoughts were interrupted by the sudden onslaught of my mother's speech.

'Bloody school inspector called out today son, I had to let on I wasn't in, he put a note through the letterbox saying he would call next Friday when you get your Christmas holidays', she said. I made no reply but noticed that her soft gentle voice shook as she pronounced each word, trying to deprive herself from sounding the alarm bells.

'Son! You're going to have to go to school a wee bit more', she said, staring out the scullery window while at the same time gathering her apron into a crumbled mess before her. 'I can't cover for you any more son, you're going to get me summonsed', she said, trying to escape my sideward glance.

I again exercised my individual right to silence, but deep inside the grotto of my childhood innocence was a rational adult preparing to murder the sentry of youth. I thought of the long spring days when every girl and boy attended the school of poisoned facts and carefully selected knowledge; when my mother and I would walk to Maghera, drowning the scarlet enemy of worry and hardship beneath the sea of newborn lambs, speeding hares and nature's assortment of rainbow flowers. How on our return with the weekly shopping we would rest beneath an oak tree older than mum herself and drink brown lemonade and eat squares of rich creamy chocolate, as we surveyed the passing roar of Hillmans, Morris Minors and Mini cars. I thought of the cold winter days when I huddled up close to the warm turf fire when mum recalled her glory days of childhood happiness and pranks, never to be forgotten. In her presence there was an Inn where I could find refuge, she understood why I loathed school and was always prepared to defend my wish to remain at home. Now it was my turn to seek and find the Inn that would accommodate the status quo.

While I pondered the idea that minds must be mangled to dry out an answer; I could hear my father's voice raise its authority above the din of noisy children.

'Shush till I hear the news'.

Among all the familiar atrocities of the time, one news item seemed to project in union with my confused state of mind.

POLICE SAY THE 58-YEAR-OLD FACTORY WORKER WHO WAS SHOT AT, BUT UNINJURED, HAS DECIDED TO LEAVE HIS PLACE OF WORK. THE CHIEF CONSTABLE IN CONDEMNING THE ATTACK SAID IT WAS CLEARLY A BLATANT SECTARIAN INTIMIDATION OF PEOPLE GOING ABOUT THEIR DAILY TOILS...

My mind blanked out the remainder of the news and contented itself to focus purely on the plan that had now emerged inside a flashing light bulb above my head. Could I in all youthful courage reach to the extreme and with one shot from James' air rifle, dilute the very thickness of my discontent? The school inspector would discontinue his imposition of wills and find another job, or perhaps crawl into the deep bottomless hole of retirement. I could see the inspector's face change from one of authority to one of terror, the mortal threat to remove my worldly allowance of happiness would soon disappear in the rear view mirror of his resignation. In the unbeknown oblivion of James' intoxicating state, I would borrow the weapon that would give to me the eraser of fate and on a day that was in keeping with my judgment, I would indulge in the act of correcting.

The solids of awakening that night were not easily broken by the hammer of slumber. I fought with the idea, changing the plan many times only to return to the original before the gateway of my conscience. In the thin musky air of my eventual dreams I stand before the headmaster, he is smiling. My fellow youngsters applaud my presence with theirs, reaching out to give praise to their redeemer. The headmaster invites me to punish him for the perpetrating crimes he has inflicted on humanity. The classroom instigates their verdict in the form of descending thumbs. I stand before them, a mirror on the hallway wall of justice. I raise the air rifle and delightfully pull the trigger, there is something wrong, it is not the headmaster who is falling before my feet, it is my mother.

 I screamed from deep within the very depths of my soul. On my departure from the classroom of horror, I see my mother's solid face soothing my delusion of terror.

'You're all right son it's just a nightmare, calm down', she said.

I had returned to reality through the thunder of my maternal calling and had only been made at ease by the bright human form that had now embraced me with soothing hush. And the realization that the bridge over the river of my contentment had not fell into the waters of despair. When my mother left, I slowly returned to the grey dreary enclosure of my dreams only to find that its emptiness had become a blessing, and awoke in the morning to the glare of a winter sun and the incarnation of a pair of hob-nail boots.

2

A TRUTH FOR EVERY SPOOF

I spent the opening of the new day coming to terms with the premeditation of my imminent crime. The urge to commit such an act was not halted in its journey by the barrier of a good night's sleep, nor the odour undesirable to my nasal sense had no relation to its foulness, but came as a direct result of my brother John's regular habit of discharging putrid thunder from an area where the sun fails to shine. Following a hurried breakfast of porridge, I decided that never was a time more convenient to pay a visit to James' modest environment. This intention I kept to myself and followed the damp grassy lane that led me once again to the entrance of Peter's farmyard. The geese had decided that following the previous day's confrontation, it was not beneficial to their health to engage me in any further acts of aggression. This lull in hostilities was greeted with thanks, allowing me free passage to proceed through thorny bushes, barbed wire, rushes, Ben weeds and the occasional encounter with cow's dung, until I stood before the rich colony of woodworm that James had opted to call the front door to his whitewashed house.

On one's first experience of the aged house, it was firmly accepted by those who valued their welfare that three loud knocks must quickly be succeeded by the rowdy passing of identification. It is also widely known that if any manifestation that did not carry out these decrees could soon find themselves the receiver of an assortment of painful lead fragments discharged from an ancient shotgun by the name of Mary Jane. As I was quite related to these facts, I carried them out with the swiftness and decisiveness required and soon found myself in the living quarters of James' habitat.

I entered during the process of James reaching to return Mary Jane to the hooks on the black oak beam that lingered above his head, and was greeted by the usual smile bearing a consortium of brown and black teeth, garnished with a side salad of empty spaces. As far back as I can return in my life, James still looked the same. From his black laced boots, grey glazed trousers, brown-buttoned jacket sheltering a maroon pullover with a hint of a not so white shirt. On his head he sported a black peak hat, with a few tresses of grey hair reclining on the trench forehead of a weather kicked face. Through the mouldy air of his enclosure, the private odour of illicit spirits took dominance over the smoke from the turf fire. Across from the bed in which he also used as a sofa stood a brown worn armchair. It was on this object of a visitor's settlement that I perched my juvenile presence and stood facing, unbeknown to himself, the promoter of my conspiracy.

'Well son', he muttered in a slurred voice, 'did ya shave tha day'?

Before I could utter any reply to this form of greeting, he threw himself into a noisy convulsion of hysterical laughter, shaking the unsteady four-poster bed and forcing the small grey mouse who had been attempting to feast on a fragment of blue moulded bread, to retreat to safety from hence it came. As quickly as the laughter had commenced it stopped, bringing the confines of James' senses back to his readiness to reflect his kindness by offering me a mixture of brown lemonade and biscuits. He then began to inflict me with a long line of jokes that my ears had now grown weary of their recognition. To his delight I joined in on the amusement, not to the funny end of the subject, but to the aspect in which he projected his laughter to the irritation of the bed and the retreating mouse. It had come to my conclusion that the bread once wore the coat of freshness, but had lately decayed without the mouse ever having the pleasure of introducing its minute palate to the focus of its craving. On my visits to James' the fun and refreshments were usually followed by the usual chores. Fetch a bucket of water, fetch the milk from a farm up the road, go to the shop for groceries and on the return journey collect several bottles of stout from Maggie's pub. All this was rewarded with a second round of the same jokes and another helping of brown lemonade and assorted biscuits. It was during this serving of refreshment that I found the situation requiring some knowledge of my future ploy, so I made the move of asking James if it was to his satisfaction, I might have a shot or two from his air gun.

'Surely son', he replied.

He then followed this request by reaching behind the old blue dresser, recovered the weapon, and produced a key that fitted the drawer and turned. The dresser's contents yelled in annoyance as he extracted a box of slugs from the swollen drawer, and placed the usual quota of five onto the palm of my hand. He then proceeded somewhat unsteadily to return the remainder back to their place of hiding. It could not be described as any way difficult to take the usual place, ten foot from the matchbox perched on top of the dry stone wall and fire. In the acceptance of my regularity, James' senses would not fodder my malignant expectations; therefore at the closing of my weekly target practice and the return of the air rifle, two slugs had taken their unruly place inside the confines of my pocket. The first letter of my plan had been truly sealed.

As I took my departure from James' I made my way down the clean tar lane, over uneven footing of spent potato drills, across the back of high ground saturated by thriving fir trees and onto a place that breathed the air of mystic quality. Before me on that raw Saturday morning stood my refuge from all sorrow. A broad stone solitary wall moulded in unison with the grey sky and shrouded by a thick layer of green moss. James had once told me on one of his rare sober frames of mind, that a cottage once stood, where an old woman who was said to be a hundred years old lived and possessed the gift to cure bleeding hearts. She was thought to have extracted the sorrows of others and placed their heavy burden into her own heart. Her end came in the early hours of a Good

Friday morning when the countryside was awakened to the wailing of a thousand deaths. It was some time before anyone dared to venture up, only to discover that the cottage had disappeared leaving behind one wall protected by a shield of emerald green moss. It was here that truancy had invited me to abide and on the mornings prior to the realization of the only option available to squash the school inspector's conviction, in my yearning for stability, I replaced wrong with right. From the wall I used to envy the towering mountains of The Glen Shane, that dominated the Derry landscape. The eerie mist now forged with the fumes of passing traffic to cushion the sky with hope. In the presence of nature the treetops bowed to the royalty of the north wind, a cold wind that did not dare trespass on the moss wall. It was also here at this very wall that in my remote thoughts I stirred the past with the future, and wondered what brush the artist of time would carefully portray my destiny. I have often trespassed on the forth field on cobwebbed mid-summer nights, to seek out the tiny mythical minds of fairy souls, only to be rewarded by the smell of murdered hay and the introduction of an ash-stick for staying out late. And if my puerile mind had once dared to doubt the fairy's presence, my shadow would indeed have vanished before the feet of a falling virtue. If I had replaced the drawl of textbooks and ballpoint pens with wisdom from the common mind, then it was by fate and by fate alone. From the septic clutches of the classroom, I had been snatched by the teachers of life. My words were now read from the faces of righteous women and men, my letters I now inscribed on the parchment of their souls.

When I took leave of my thoughts, together with the moss wall, I made my way down a rustic uneven lane, past a field that sported a brown staring donkey and onto the sweet smelling heather of an open bog. In the distance reaching above my head grew Sonny's hill; upon these acres of high soil lived Sonny, a sheep farmer and a baker of unique soda scones. In his pride he had boasted the availability of the largest currants for thousands of miles, and it was some time before customers discovered that his sheep were his sole suppliers. In Sonny there was an element of amiable character that was rare in changing times. You could hear the clear tone of his singing voice for miles, an echo that even the hens hurried to give audience.

From the pulped, almost purple crevices on his face, he greeted me with cheek-lunging expression and almost immediately invited me for a sample of his prized scones. The morning portion of porridge had by now been defeated by the more aggressive hunger, but to my stomach's utter horror, I declined on the false grounds of having eaten heartily beforehand. A perjury that was well orchestrated to be in keeping with the present circumstances.

'Yous youngins now doesn't know what's good for em', he muttered in defeat, 'sure a hell they'll come a day when they'll be queuing up for miles just for a sniff of Sonny's soda scones'.

I assured him that, that would most certainly be the case and muttered in humorous agreement when he stated that the sheep had become a nuisance, and due to the fall in demand for soda scones, their services would no longer be required. Through the turmoil of Sonny's complaints I had failed to notice the absence of Shep, Sonny's obedient sheepdog and patient forbearer of Sonny's mentality. It was with this foremost in my reason for attendance, so I blurted out and inquired into his welfare. It was then for the first time that I bore witness to Sonny's clear expression, now being mangled in the cogs of sorrow.

'Ah Shep has decided to leave us', he muttered, 'gone these last three days and no sign of the blurt anywhere'.

'How did this come about?' I asked in an alarming voice.

'Don't know', replied Sonny, 'got up Thursday morning, went to the barn where he sleeps and found nothing but a lonely bone'. I informed him that the possibility of thieves lurking in the night had most likely played a major role in Shep's disappearance, in which he replied.

'No son, last band that decided to play around here late at night received the nasty end of my single barrel; they wouldn't try a second time'.

Several possibilities now scavenged my mind for reason. Perhaps Shep had wandered off at night and had been the victim of someone else's single barrel? Perhaps his senses had taken their leave and he was now lost in some dark field of bewilderment? But more likely against Sonny's own judgment on the situation, the thieves had boldly grasped the hand of defiance and removed the faithful Shep from under Sonny's very snores. By removing Shep, the culprits had taken away Sonny's very flame of worldly warmth. No longer would the morning sun dominate the new day, nor the short familiar bark coupled by the rhythm of Shep's tail be a mascot on Sonny's peppered stone yard.

As he turned to take the short incline back to the cavity of his home, I could only stare helplessly at the broken remnant of pity and hope and pray that somehow Sonny would be reunited with his canine companion. As these thoughts weighed heavily on my heart, Sonny suddenly stopped on the path of his departure, waited a few seconds then turned and spoke.

'Twenty pound for the mutt's return', he said in a loud voice. It did not escape me for long that as I was the only other earthly being apparent to the moment, these words were flung directly at me, forcefully like a thud from a hard grey rock. And I took an even shorter course to come to the conclusion, in which I sprang with contempt to my dire defence.

'How dare you Sonny', I cried, 'how dare you blame me for stealing Shep'.

It was at the conclusion of these angry words and owing to the fact that I had not yet reached the stage of adolescence; the optical rivers began to flow on their grieving journey down my artless features. In my wounded state of turbulent innocence I began to run. To run with the intention of freeing myself forever from the offending Sonny, and vowing with bitterness to never cross his path again, on mortal or immortal ground.

If the miles before me had equalled one hundred in length, I would have banished every thought of their distance and perhaps collapsed exhausted in death.

But whether the deep bog hole had been designed as an obstacle to further reduce me in spirit, I will never apprehend. All I can recall at that harrowing and terrifying moment was my small body being engulfed by the dark putrid mass of bog water. As I sank deeper and deeper into the darkness, I could see the light disappear beyond the gorge of liquid death, and my page of destiny had now appeared in the hands of my own ghost. Through the perpetual tunnel which leads to my soul, a bell beckons me to venture within. I am wary of the objectives of the frozen tolls and prepare from the core of my frantic awareness, to smash the breathing mirror of bereavement. In a moment between the oblivious line, I am returned to solid ground with one hurried greeting of light. I feel the warm secure hands of human touch; I am with life once again and quickly drift off into the feathered softness of forced sleep.

In atonement for my stupidity I am affected to bear the weight of my short sightedness when reality returns to clothe my naked shame. Awake beside an old wood burn stove and wrapped in a thick wool blanket, I stare into the eyes of my saviour. The tired eyes of Sonny's stare had forced me to grasp the burning fact that he indeed had come to my aid in my fatal minutes and after wrenching me from the molars of extinction, had laboriously carried me to the comfort of his home. The realization of the moments leading up to the accident had fallen on my mind's lap like a mountain of molten rocks. I could only cry out in relayed words that I had not dared remove Shep from his fondness, and would never have fashioned such a deed even in my blackest dreams.

'Now, now son', said Sonny, softly patting me on the head, 'don't tear yourself ta bits over that'.

He began to explain to me what his real intention was behind the statement. While he was making his way back to his house, by accidental observance and completely unrelated to the topic, he managed to steal a view towards the hawthorn hedge and low and behold he caught a quick glimpse of someone's peak cap descending below the hedge line, in order to escape his scope. Reassuring his thoughts that this person or persons were in no way eager to join the conversation, he decided that a reward of hard currency was music to the ears of those with villainous objectives. And that those who had taken it upon themselves to remain concealed for obvious reasons known only to themselves, may have information that might lead to the return of the faithful Shep. As he had more knowledge of the layout of the local landscape than myself, he decided that to pursue me when I had taken off like a wounded hare would be beneficial to my well-being, and in doing so he had freed me from the dungeons of drowning.

I could not apologise enough to Sonny on hearing his explanation. He shrugged it off with the modesty and humble embarrassment relative to rural simplicity and decided while my clothes dried above the fire range, nothing less than a yes could be considered when he decided that I should have a cup of tea, with a freshly baked soda scone. I was in no position to defend any declining of his offer, so with mind and mouth agape I watched helplessly as Sonny prepared his famous meal. I stared in amazement as Sonny first mixed the dough in a large white bowl; he then fetched a jar of the horrid currants and emptied half of its contents into the mixture.

'Just a few dried plums with the stones removed son', he said. And sure enough after closer observation, I discovered that in all truth they were indeed plums. After separating the dough into small round shapes he then proceeded to make his way to the back door. A few minutes later he returned with a grey tin bucket containing an abundance of dried sheep's stools.

'Nothing like dried dung to burn an even temperature', he said.
And following these words opened the stove's cast-iron door and deposited some of the matter into the fire.

In that few moments the truth of Sonny's character had been given no comfort by the fact that other men's minds and vindictiveness had seriously blemished the skill and art of Sonny's baking skills. As I consumed the generous helpings of soda bread that were placed before me, I deported all rumours that had been illegally employed to inflict a great wrong on a gigantic right. It was also my second intention as I swallowed the last morsel and drained my cup that with my uppermost help, Sonny's integrity as a baker would be returned. My first intention was to seek out the culprits who had removed Sonny's dog from the contentment of its warm dry barn. In all fairness Sonny had been beat by the undeserving stick, and if good is destined to obliterate all that is bad, then that stick must be broken in several places. As I dressed myself in the parch fabric of my clothing, I could not remove the tearing thought that dragged behind my worldly happiness. In the near future the eroding harm that was weakening my mast of peace would have to be removed. Through the burning haystacks of my vengeance the school inspector's spectre would smoulder. His authority and daydreams of child dominance would be lost in the ashes of fear.

As I departed from Sonny's unforgettable hospitality, I quickly found my way home. I was soon greeted by Jip and the calling aroma of mother's cooking, who both led me to the back door of my material asylum. As I sat down at the old oak table, I thanked mum for her hearty display of bacon, cabbage and blue potatoes. I decided that in both our interests no rundown of the day's events need be forthwith. As it had now become closer to the destination of darkness, I was advised by my mother on completion of my meal that my father's presence would soon become a familiar fact, and to be in union with my bodily welfare I should hurry to bed.

As I positioned myself under the crisp cold blankets of my bottom bunk bed, my brother John had already preceded me some moments earlier, and was overly anxious that I fodder his intrusive mind on episodes prior to my present situation. With minor reluctance, I began to recite my own version of events, with extracts not relevant to the wiser older brother, omitted from the script. It had become a common practice in the seclusion of our room, that following the day's adventures, I would recite stories of my own creation in the hope that sooner, rather than later,

John's impersonating of a swine would dominate the musty air. On the realization of his slumber I would call off the bedtime story and once again return to the drawing board of my plan, the plan that would steer me closer to the conclusion of my voyage.

3

SUNDAY HATS AND TROUBLE MAKING RATS

Like most Sunday mornings in conjunction with my span of life, I awoke to the carnage of my four elder sisters returning from early mass. It was this that signalled me to the circumstance that my brother John and myself must don our Sabbath masks and angelically walk the short distance to the local chapel. At our approach to the tall grey tower of duty the road was characterized by terraced trees spanning both sides of the road. It was here we had become accustomed to rendering our positions on the middle of the road to prevent crows from deciding to inflict the call of nature onto our immaculate attire. It had become commonplace for those completely forgetful of the calamity that rained down from above, and after realizing, angrily reciting vocabulary that our immature minds were unable to fathom. Words that to the more learned were unbecoming to their destination.

As we entered the vast enclosure of the church, the

first ritual leading up to the celebration of mass was the inspection. For many years it was a custom among the local gathering that the dress code and identification must be asserted at all times. This usually began with hundreds of gawking perfectionists bending in unison to the shoes, slowly up to the trousers and last but not least, the upper garments. On passing this autopsy we made our way past the chocolate coloured pews, ascended the wooden steps noisily onto the gallery, and took a seat at the front row in order that my brother John might engage the soft choral voice of the choir, in the act of rasping hostility.

At the entrance of Father Pat, the mass of people quickly rose, allowing the impression of a head of hair being subjected to a gluttonous quota of electricity. At the point of our kneeling I began to take more notice of the old priest as he struggled to make his way up the three short steps that would take him to the altar. His days of retirement were quickly approaching and my heart moved in reminiscence as I thought of the days when I had been chosen as an altar boy to clerk the stations held in private houses. The subject was one that was firmly etched with admiration for the aged curate. At the dinner table post proceedings, I was positioned at his right hand and with extreme amusement to himself, received portions of top of the league nourishment over abundant to my magnitude. In his eyes I had become no inferior than a King, and on Christmas days had been awarded with a crisp green pound which I happily presented to my mother to ease the wanton chains of monetary yearning.

It was during the first chorus sung by the choir and to my amazement, my brother John produced from his pocket, what could only be described as a five inch steel bolt complete with washer and nut. It was to my even greater amazement when he decided to divorce the object and send it spinning in horrid rotation over the saintly edge of the balcony. And in the confusion, I am ashamed to say that on reaching its unpredicted destination, a voice much superior in tone and alto than the songsters on the upper deck, had now taking precedence over the closing hymn. I have to say once again that if the assault had have been inflicted under alternative momentary lodgings, lyrics of a more tasteless nature would have most certainly been applied. It was not long following this unholy deed that a man applying a handkerchief to an egg sized object on his forehead departed, refusing to have anymore participation in the remainder of the Sabbath proceedings. And on our way back from Holy Communion as we normally did, John and I on passing the door, exited and started out prematurely on our way home.

The sacrilegious assault carried out some moments before had by no means been an isolated incident, in either John's or my self's portion of existence. As boys will most certainly claim that entitlement, Halloween a few weeks earlier had not been left untainted by our wickedness.

When it had come to the brink of that particular time of the year when most people rued the approaching of innocent torture, youth throughout every generation sadistically find an excuse to threaten their elders into submission. Or the insolent swear from both man and woman, whose only aggravation was to crack nuts on teeth that were well past their sell by date. On Halloween nights we would roast chestnuts on the fire until they were so badly cremated, nothing remained of the ashes. And around this very fire we would brew up the scheming, sniffling, unrepentant premeditated wickedness that boiled within our innocent minds. One misleading task that became an annual event was to draw straws to select a loser, the loser then had to perform whatever act of tyranny that was forced upon him, usually by the older boys. Like all boys of moral stature, they were well apprenticed in the art of deceit, so I in my solitary naivety became the annual washout.

The task that was selected at hand was to steal up to Peter the farmer's door, take the necessary steps backwards in order to obtain an acceptable strike, charge forward in the best possible manner and apply footwear with as much force that was mandatory to awaken Peter from his much deserved repose beside the cast-iron stove. Nine times out of ten this would result in a two or three mile pursuit across half dug potato fields, over barbed wire fences and ending in Peter's body being inhumanely demoralized in four foot of freezing water.

I proceeded to carry out the instructions that the older boys had laid before me, and also to test my new black laced boots for durability. I decided that an impression on the older boys was vital to win their recognition, so a few extra paces backwards were required in the hope that Peter didn't miss out on the fun also. So low and behold, I gathered my courage into one small ball of breathing flesh and made the great white dash of chivalry. As I approached Peter's door with the speed I prided myself in achieving, I plunged the necessary limb at the green aged wooden door, hoping to carry out my task with firm effectiveness. To my unexpected horror that could only be accredited to a Halloween night, a large gaping hole appeared around the thrusting footwear, leaving ample space for the rest of the limb to wedge tightly and surrendering me to the disposal of Peter's semi-conscious unforgiving repugnance.

Owing to the infliction of similar pains against the persecuted Peter, I did not expect to receive any clemency. The older boys including the blood relative brother John had decided to take their leave in an accelerated manner that would have made N.A.S.A.'s rocket ship resemble a hot air balloon. I remained solitary to the night with a fortitude that could only be becoming to the present situation, and as I turned my head to face the victorious Peter, the tears were already saturating the grey stone floor.

If the angel of remorse had indeed flown above me in that closing October night, or somehow the scriptwriter of fate had lost the closing page, I will never know. All that became clear in my memory is that in Peter's insane engagement of vengeance, the new ensnared black laced boot had somehow been removed from its appendage, allowing me to swiftly retrieve my trapped limb. Much to Peter's despair, the dark coarse blackthorn stick that had been employed for the destruction of my well being, was now raining down on an empty abandoned item of footwear. Much of what was to be expected, I claimed an angry oral assault from my mother's frustrated cry, informing me that I should not have removed my boots to dry my feet, especially when one was destined to smother among the flames.

On our return from Sunday worship, a glimpse of my mother leaning out the kitchen window with a double barrel shotgun, reminded me once again of the festered times that had dominated an Ulster existence. The reality of the situation at hand, I could well describe as clear in every aspect. These windows of insight can be contributed mostly to the failure of the adult mind to recognize the aptitude of the minor intellect, and that childhood awareness can be much superior than a jam sandwich, or ten pence for sweets. Years prior to the momentary event, Civil Rights campaigners advanced in defiance to the tune of 'We Shall Overcome'. My recollections at the sight of these insubordinates were mixed in a bowl of fear and curiosity, and at a time when the air could have been convicted as cleaner, a few extra gasps were inhaled in excitation. Among all the vocabulary of the time were words like 'Burn Out', 'Dead' and 'Beaten', words that were easily translated by my brother John who was personally educated by films like 'Gunfight At The O.K. Corral and 'Jessie James', as spelling danger. In his own description of these meanings, one could be left with nothing shorter than the feeling of unmitigated terror.

It had come to my intention following a few carefully

selected questions and observations that trouble had flared during a mass strike. For those on one side of the religious divide or the other, threats to their territorial situations were to be taken seriously and the guarding of these positions could not be left in the hands of the optimistic. My mother had chosen to retain the act of sentry, while the optimistic played his part more modestly at the local pub.

It was my brother John who came to the conclusion that in order that we might play a crucial part in the troubled proceedings, a place of refuge must be found or constructed. As soon as any disturbance posed a threat to our humble subsistence, we could hide until the threat had subsided. So we gallantly made our way to the top of the back garden and with little or no observation of our options, decided to dig an underground bunker. We proceeded to excavate a large hole, which with intensity and fury was not completed until late in the evening. We then proceeded to cover the hole with branches borrowed from a nearby tree; this was followed up with two old potato sacks and garnished with several shovels of loose soil. The remainder of the soil was kindly donated to a nearby manhole and last but not least, we tested the strength of the cover over the aperture and congratulated ourselves on a job well done.

By the time we finished our day's work the winter darkness had arrived uninvited, allowing no space for those with lesser eyesight. As bedtime was inevitable, we hungrily consumed our supper and stared around the interior of the silent household. An air of change had now descended, smothering the traditional childish mayhem under a blanket of fear. The aged black and white television that often required several Karate chops on its head in order to give some stability to the picture, now joined the silence of the moment. And however much the stove was abundantly foddered with fuel, I could still feel a shiver taking it upon itself to crawl in rapturous motion down my spine. Jip the family dog stared at us through glazed eyes, waiting patiently for the left over crusts of bread from supper.

At the hour of slumber we made our way slowly to our place of rest and as we recited a bedtime prayer with mum, an aria of urgency hang over every word like a requiem for lost souls. It took some time before I could embrace the appreciation of sleep and the long roadway to dawn was haunted with terrible dreams, of Indians invading the house, of dead Cowboys and long dark strange shadows hanging over every wall.

Dawn eventually arrived in the form of a loud explosion, and with my heart frantically trying to escape up my throat; I jumped out of the bunk bed as was planned the previous day. I discovered that my brother John had decided to disembark at the same moment, allowing his body to have the pleasure of a soft landing at the painful expense of my bruised self. Another thunderous explosion could be heard followed almost instantly by the sound of shattered glass, and it was then that full and complete mayhem imposed itself on the morning household. As we hurried out the room door, I caught a glimpse of my mother aiming a smoking shotgun in the general direction of the bathroom window. As we proceeded to exit by the back door I could see my father dressed in his oversized vest and long johns, running excitingly up the back garden and without reservation disappear into the ground. He then as he was lawfully entitled to do so under the present circumstances, begin to curse anything and everything that was not above the sun. From within the confusion, John suddenly pointed to an oversized rat that decided to take upon itself to stare at us without fear from a bundle of loose stones. Owing to this discovery and the folding of the script of turmoil, the facts began to emerge from their place of hiding.

While my mother was paying her regular morning visit to the bathroom, she spied the rat and took it upon herself that she would make the best candidate to erase the trespasser from its vermin existence. She, not being what my brother John would call a sharp shooter, missed and removed most of the window glass in the process. My father being in chauvinist contempt at my mother's offside shot, decided to pursue the monster and complete the chore with his bare hands. With the inevitable about to happen, he stepped on the construction tested by those of a flimsier weight and without any worldly warning, descended to what he must have thought of at the time as hell.

My brother and I with soft and gentle innocence, denied any knowledge of the monstrosity that took so long to construct and as we sat down to breakfast that morning, a feeling of relief crawled across our fear crushing it with contentment. The black and white television shone pictures of moving glee; the stove leaning against the cream peppered wall, although almost extinguished, reflected more heat than usual. And Jip the black and brown canine bundle of hair lay fast asleep beneath the chocolate wood sideboard.

4

A DOVE FROM ABOVE

The delights of the morning's peacefulness were soon poisoned by the realization that Monday refused to deny that the dreaded classroom was inevitable. My brother John had already departed to catch the bus for Stony High School and without forwarding a challenge to my mother's insistence; I reached for the brown leather bag and set off down the familiar path of persecution. I had given no claim to the fact that all must be persevered until the mallet of departure slammed down on the ending of my primary school days. I had taken an oath, often whispered in the clear confinements of my judgment and that oath I would carry to the top, however solid and burdensome it may be. It now being the last week before Christmas snatched me from my unholy internment; I would carefully unwind my conscience and grasp the hand of my principles with an honourable glove. The road to school had now become a destination to Calvary and with my heavy cross; I slowly walked to my crucifixion.

In all probability the classroom would not in the least bit falter from its frosty compassion. The weekend's hibernation may have added to the dairy of my recollections, but these pages were insistently lacerated by the closing sword of the last few days. My sordid chair is obediently taken, my being turns quickly away from my agony and the treacherous drawing pins bear no grudge on my earthly flesh. The clicking feet that approach from the polished corridor sell me no recognition. The turning of inquisitive heads does no justice to the branded custom, nor does the small, lean, unfamiliar image that breached the classroom door.

I am wide-awake, yet I reverie among the immortal clouds. The dark brown pinstripe skirt twins with the jacket, higher up the brown narrowly bleaches to form the smooth skin of a heavenly face, a face the artist of life allowed for two deep blue crystal eyes. As she surveys the surrounding visions of bewilderment, her long silky charcoal hair moves slowly to fan her fiery presence with spirited breath. I am once again running through the flowers of summer scent, my heart beats wildly from within my breathless breast and from the red rose lips of refuge I hear the voice of truth.

'Good Morning girls and boys', she said. 'my name is Angelica Martin; you may call me Miss Martin'.
She moved her stare around the classroom and smiled, 'I am a student teacher and all this week and into the New Year, I will have the very greatest pleasure of teaching you all', she said, 'I hope we all get on extremely well together'.
From the echo of her voice floating in sincerity

around the room, I knew that her wish would be granted. I also knew that Angelica had been sent as an angel of mercy to shine some hope into my darkest week. By her nearness I had now become ripe, hanging from the tree of civil identity.

She spoke again, 'Is Oliver Mckenna in the class, if he is could he please put his hand up'. At my Christian recognition I slowly abided by her demand and raised my hand high into the now perfumed air.

'Oliver, would you please remain behind at break time', she said, 'I would like a few discreet words alone'.

'Yes Miss Martin', I found myself replying.

I was so stunned by this request that some minutes later the soft voice assured me that it was safe to take my hand down.

I had no solid ingredients brewing in the vats of my mind to suggest why Miss Martin had signalled me out. When the bell rang at ten o clock I remained in my seat, almost obliterated by inquisitive leers from the departing youngsters and at her beckoning, separated from my chair and moved obediently to a position before her desk.

'Now Oliver', she said, 'your headmaster has advised me that it is in your nature to be an irregular attendee of school. In addition he has also brought to my attention that you are a disruptive and troublesome boy, who will stop at nothing to cause havoc among your fellow pupils, what have you to say for yourself?'

The ease in which I sprang to my own defence had indeed somewhat baffled my own capabilities. I informed Miss Martin in the clearest of language that

I indeed was a victim, bullied and taunted into taking action that was in keeping with my temperament. If I had verily taken allowance, much more than what is acceptable, then the circumstances in which I had described were as a direct result. I also informed her without reservation and in words to that effect, that the headmaster's daydreams of child dominance were extreme in their making, and went far beyond the fringes of cruelty. I had no wish whatsoever of depriving myself of the right to be educated, but on the scales of human tolerance, absence fell heavily to the ground.

Following my deliberation and the few minutes it took Miss Martin to digest the storming of my words, she spoke again with what I perceived was an expanded caring voice.

'Would you like to have your break with me?' I informed her that eating food at ten o clock was as familiar to me as the surface of the moon and with all due respect, would not deprive her of that pleasure.

'Well then Oliver', she said, 'you can share mine, I'm not the world's greatest vulture and I don't like the word waste'.

With no, most definitely not allowed for an answer, I sat down and enjoyed ham and pickle sandwiches for the first time and thanked Miss Martin most hungrily for her thoughtfulness. On completion of this savoury task, Miss Martin then reached into the drawer of the desk and produced the object of my punishment.

'Do you know what this is?' she smiled.

I informed her that from the first day on entering this classroom I had become only too familiar with the bamboo object in question.

'Well Oliver', she replied, 'take it in your hands and break it'. I could only stand agape before the request that surely had been removed from the book of madness, an expression that allowed Miss Martin to reflect an even greater display of pleasure.

'Well then', she said, 'if you won't then I will just have to do it myself'.

She then proceeded to grasp the cane in both hands and following a loud crack over her knee; she broke the enemy's back in one swift assault.

'There will be no need for punishment in my class', she said, 'I will meet you with honour half road'.

With some difficulty in hiding my emotions, I acquainted her with the knowledge that on my part, that road of honour would be completed to the end and that only the respect that she deserved was forthcoming.

As Miss Martin addressed the class on their return from break, I could only awe at the circumstance that had now carried itself into the classroom. I had now somewhat renewed my faith in education, but in silent dread I knew the return of the headmaster was inevitable. For these short days of contentment would quickly vanish, and the brightness would once again be replaced by the epoch of darkness. In her sermon to the contents of the classroom, she preached the sins of bullying and neighbourly hostility. She bellowed the act of tolerance within our puerile confinement and ended with friendship from the cot to the grave. That friendship forged on the school days anvil would carry us through our turbulent stations of life and must be cherished, regardless of how far we are forced to wander.

At the interval relevant to our hunger, I sat at the dinner table both mentally and physically unscathed. From the watchful eyes of Miss Martin I consumed my generous helping of sausages, potatoes and peas, followed by a healthy bowl of rice pudding. During these two occasions my guardian angel inflicted upon me extra helpings of the same and at the closing of this most ravenous celebration, the walk back to the classroom was severely hampered by the internal baggage.

On my return to my desk I was greatly surprised to find that my table had now sported the very best in contemporary learning materials. These consisted of jotter, two pencils, exercise book and a bright glossy hardback children's novel. Through the envy of my school colleagues I thanked Miss Martin most dearly for her generosity, and insisted on inscribing my name carefully on the front of each cover in case of over covetous resentful pupils. I had now been reinstated among those eager to learn and perhaps without any unforeseen icebergs, and with the help of Miss Martin, I might one day be placed upon the high social stool.

Throughout the remainder of the day I sat transfixed, engrossed in the words floating like candy floss from the mouth of Miss Martin. Words that were read for our afternoon story and one of many stories that would fertilize the fields of my mind in preparation for the great harvests of life.

As I made my way home through the chill of the evening, I could safely say with mild embarrassment that I was disappointed that the school day had now come to a conclusion. The familiar quickening of my pace had now been faltered by the magnet of fondness that Miss Martin had aimed in my direction unexpectedly. As I entered through the back door of my home, my mother had commented in absolute astonishment, at my unusual belated attendance for tea. Through the crack in the kitchen door, I caught her stare at the rarity of my change of attitude.

With the thoughts of the adorable Miss Martin momentary dissolved from my thoughts and at the request from my mother, I made my way on an errand to the local shop which calculated about a mile from the beginning of my journey. A note with the list of requirements was planted safely in my pocket and with the absence of currency; the common request for credit would have to be employed on this occasion. It was not at all rare for families with meagre backgrounds to adopt this method of humility. With the high unemployment and wages well below the national average, families and shopkeepers alike bore no grudges on this method of doing business. In order to sooth the bruise of this bashful errand, a quarter of Merry Maid toffees were also included in the list.

When I opened the red wooden door of Sandy's old shop, the aged hinges cried out in eroded contempt. When I reflect on the word old, I have no doubt by the appearance of the cramped establishment, that old was the appropriate word. Through the musty smell of tobacco, blended with the aroma of varies sweets and goods, Sandy greeted my youthful being by exposing a toothless grin. Being thankful for the scarcity of customers, I hurriedly handed over the dreaded note and stepped back from the woodworm counter to await the verdict. At the revelation of the contents, Sandy's expression was hurriedly withdrawn back to fort, and before he could mutter another word, the door was flung violently open admitting another customer in the form of a farmer, by the name of Jack Keirn. As my eyes proceeded to take in the frame of the unwelcome Jack, I noticed that in unification with the folded down Wellington boots, blue dung-stained overalls and peak cap, he was excitingly out of breath. Gasping for enough oxygen in which to call out his order, he eventually spoke in a quick exasperated language.

'Hello Sandy, quick givis a ha pound of coul am, a plain bread loaf and a pacic of marroh root bickies'.

With an attitude that this type of event was entirely unfamiliar to the sober Sandy, he proceeded to accommodate Jack in keeping with his leisure. After the lengthy act of fetching the items and laying them before the in a hurry farmer, Jack spoke again.

'A tin of them there red beans', he gasped, 'Packy likes a bean way ese spud'.

On his way to fetch the second request, Sandy suddenly stopped, turned around to Jack and spoke.

'My garters Jack, ya seem ta be a host out a breath', he said.

'Ah don't tak', replied Jack, 'if you had twenty-seven cows ta horn from seven o'clock tha morning surely you would be done', he wheezed.

On contemplation to this reply, Sandy decided that in

the best interests of morality, the subject would not be worth pursuing and continued to fetch the requirements of Jack the farmer.

As it took some considerable time for the two to negotiate their business, I had to wait beside a rust stained oil barrel within the shop that was still used for distributing paraffin oil. Unaware of the dangers in my midst, I rested my hand on top of the ancient contraption and with the same hand somewhat disorientated, I quickly retrieved it bearing the digested remainders of Sandy's grey cat's dinner. I was also nauseatingly made aware that some of the feline excrement had taken refuge on jack's plain bread loaf.

At the wake of Jack's departure, Sandy began depositing the contents of the note into two plastic carrying bags, and with as much enthusiasm as a pick pocket, began to copy each item into a thick black ledger. On his returning the list of I.O.U.'s to whence it came, I departed from the shop and began to labour my way home, stopping occasionally to deposit a thick chocolate and toffee sweet into the cavity of my mouth.

5

MORTAL THUNDERS AND UNHOLY BLUNDERS

During the coming days, school for me had become as welcome as the prodigal son had been to his father. Angelica had placed me close to her attention and I began to form words from the cobwebs that I formerly made with a pencil. Every footstep, every movement however small and every word that fluttered from the crevice of Angelica's mouth were harnessed tightly in the stables of my infatuation. I had now become smothered in her purity, indebted to her honesty and above all, I was now welded to her presence. The virtue of human kindness and compassion had bleached the colour of my vengeance, and as I quickly dressed for school that Friday morning, the day I had chosen to pay hostilities to the school inspector, I no longer possessed the space to bear hate within my heart. I would no longer grasp the sordid hand of evil nor injure my fellow child or man, either mentally or physically. And as I approached the joy soaked classroom of my beloved school, I swore that from this very moment to the closing of my entity, I would foster only righteous thoughts.

If I were to describe whole heartily the shock that sadistically greeted me as I entered the classroom, the word nuclear would have been a serious understatement. For there, perched on the chair behind Angelica's desk, sat the growl rogue figure of the dreaded headmaster, blotched like an oil stain on a Persian carpet. And I, a body of gutted hope was forced to pay treachery with my fortune of happiness; forced by dark unseen forces to wear the crown of undeserved thorns. I could not acquaint myself with the fact that my angel of mercy would embrace me no more with her heavenly presence. Did I begin to acknowledge that the past week had been some kind of illusion, created by my subconscious yearning for change? Had I been truly conjured by the magicians of providence and left to stand under the volcano of molten promises? Did I in all hideous stupidity, slip into the gorge of other men's rages?

As all these thoughts paid host to my confusion, devastated I turned and departed from the classroom, stalling only to punish the grey school corridor wall with my tiny white knuckles. The mundane air of escape greeted me once more as I collapsed gasping for life's breath beside the tall oak tree that had become an umbrella from the showers of rain on my days of strolling in inclement weather. There was no rain or howling wind now to hide the shattering of my will. Without restraint I mourned for the death of my childhood and wept for a vision that mine eyes would never see. Did I persist too willingly with my expectations, when normality descended upon the classroom in the form of Angelica? Perhaps in some silent corner of my thoughts, hope was still a worthy cause.

As I slowly gathered together the fragments of my valiant composure, I returned wholly to my pre-predicament and hung frantically to my surprise for the school inspector. The oath that I had joined together earlier in holy matrimony had now become divorced and today in my own Christian way, action would replace the vase of flowery thoughts.

As I made my way through James's open door, nothing had changed. The mouse still tried in vain to devour the crust of blue moulded bread. The cold musty damp smell cringed in unison with James's snores, and Mary Jane still hung from two rusty nails from the black oak beam hovering above. With a molar of fear biting into the pit of my stomach, I tiptoed my way to the air rifle's place of confinement behind the dresser, and reached in amidst the cobwebs and decaying wallpaper, and quietly withdrew the weapon that would administer the justice that my pain so richly deserved. The two borrowed slugs were still lying dormant within the confines of my jeans pocket, for I had no wish to give them up, regardless of the previous circumstances. I also knew that as I departed through James's front and only door, that the clock was moving faster than my mind and if I was to reach the required spot for the ambush, I would have to hurry.

For discovery's sake I dare not travel the open side roads and lanes that would lead me to my destination.

I decided to move unseen behind the trees and blackthorn hedges until I came upon a height of rock and fresh green smelling ferns, a position that stared out into the open view of the main village road. Following taking up my position among the concealment of the ferns, I removed a pellet from my pocket, broke the air rifle down and placed the ammunition into its intended place. With the rifle loaded and at the ready, I lay flat on the cold wet surface and braced myself for the coming of the enemy.

In the fusing together of my thoughts once again, I considered the moment an approbate time for my conscience to remain absent. My common sense was also barred from the present proceedings. My only object was to free myself from the scholarly curse, to rid myself from the rash of authority and begin the New Year in dignified resolution.

As the seconds slowly passed, the motorized purr of an approaching car snatched the silence from beneath the charcoal-coloured sky. From the interior of my chest, my heart began to hammer the drums of approaching danger. I began to vibrate uncontrollably as the blue Ford Cortina of recognition began to glide towards me like a phantom hearse. Still trembling, I rose to my knees, took hold firmly of my intent and positioned the rifle in the general direction of what I had now come to terms as my enemy.

The sharp screech of brakes momentarily bathed me in the sludge of disarray; my blood began to gush through my veins like the violence of a high waterfall.

I am on my feet now; the school inspector's arm reaches out from the protective cover of the open car door, and quickly begins to deliver thunder and lightning from a short stick-like object protruding from his hand.

If reality in all its foulness had revealed to me only the splinters of truth, I would indeed be viewing the school inspector's wraith at this very moment through an enduring lens. Being only in the tenth year of existence, I had borne no facts within my immaturity. The rifle dropped from my terrified hands, I turned allowing movement to return to my paralyzed limbs and began to run.

I ran through the trees and blackthorn bushes, over stone hedges and onto grassy lanes with the wildness of fear beating my ears with its madness. I ran until the roads and fields were once my spirit tread belonged no more to my recognition. I flew until the only destination that laid claim to my present senses was anywhere, far from the presence of time. I had no doubt, as a result of the vast rush of sensibility that chocked me with remorse, that I had committed a wrong against both God and man. As I fell physically and mentally exhausted and unable to move another inch, unable to fight the shroud of blackness that moved across the window of my vision. I now lay helpless, gasping for mercy from the clutches of mortal and immortal vengeance.

6

A BREATH FOR EVERY DEATH

When my senses eventually broke free from the
chains of oblivion, the sharp wrenching pain that
gripped my side would have to claim responsibility
for that hasty return. The gory sticky feeling that
leached my hand, removed any doubt of my present
predicament. Agony had again returned in fatal
fashion, as a result of a lightening blow from the hand
of the school inspector. If I had but one freedom to
choose my destiny, the discrimination and pain of the
classroom would be endured in place of my instant
anxiety, and the school inspector's threat would have
been equally invalid as the declaration of war I had
presented to my enemies. As I acquired a look at my
surroundings, I shrugged off the flickering of a turf
fire for a view at the long tresses of red hair that
moved back and forward on an old armchair beside
the same.

If I was allowed to chose only one word to describe
the features of the female form that accompanied me
inside the small dark room, the word strange would

have to be applied for the want of a better one. In addition to her long glittering red hair, deep green eyes and plum lips, the deep lines and lumps that were applied to the creation of her face were unreal and extreme in the making. There, sitting before me in a room God only knew where, were the hands, neckline and body of a beautiful young lady whose face bore the etchings of centuries of age. Among the few items that give expression to the room, was a large oak table smothered by numerous small crockery bottles, the contents known only to the imagination. If I had have been in a more clearer lodging, I may have been more insistent on prying, but from within the confines of my present plight, the low soft voice of a child renders my ears echoing as she turns from her rocking chair and speaks.

'Hello Oliver and how are you feeling?'

The voice that spoke offered me no recognition, yet in the childlike softness that was steeped in innocence and purity, there were mundane droplets that were splashed in my own being. If I had to stamp any familiarity on its certainty, the voice of my mother and Angelica would be first in the making.

'Are you unable to speak?' she asked.

'No', I managed to mumble.

'Then it would be nice to hear how you are feeling, I'm sure you are feeling extremely well', she said mockingly.

If it had not been for the scalding pain from my side that forced my energy to retreat, I may have jumped to my feet and brought those very walls crumbling down with the explosion of my rage. But resolving myself with my invalid scenario, I informed her in broken and subdued language that if indeed I was feeling extremely well, I would not now be branded in agony, humiliation and fear in someone else's abode. I also informed her with deep tearing conviction, that my life, that once had the pleasure of a past and present had been soaked in the human void, leaving no room for tomorrows.

In the small room that accommodated the diluted wounded figure of youth, I began to embrace my location and reflect in blunt and bitter terms of my situation. The moments surrounding my present dilemma were only too polished in my brain. The school inspector had somehow noticed my evil intentions, applied the gallant mask and returned fire with a much superior weapon. The pain that drilled through my side, until now, had been numbed by the velocity of escape and perhaps now enshrined in the passing of hope. Life would surely depart in the acknowledgment of bloody tears. I could not come to terms as to how I came upon these present lodgings and to who the strange lady was who taunted me with normality. If I had one request offered to me before the departure of my breath, the gluttony of liquid refreshment would be foremost on my mind. The sanding of my throat and mouth by the blast of the former rush had relinquished me from all aspects of vocal defence, allowing me no voice to give flight to the sarcasms of the lady with the red hair.

'Would you like a drink Oliver?' asked the lady
I was taken unexpected by this trespass on the garden of my thoughts that the only answer my thirst allowed, was to accept with gratefulness. My officious mind was hurriedly reconciled when the lady

in question reached for one of the crockery bottles, removed a cork stopper and handed it to me with a taunting smile still registered on her aged face. I reached out with the weakness of my limb, thanked her under my breath most desirously and poured the contents greedily into my mouth, allowing the liquid to flow fast down my throat and into the emptiness of my stomach.

If my throat had not been easily deceived I might have allowed my nostrils to decline the offer on the grounds of human endurance. The terrible stench that ascended from the bottle allowed no mercy for unawareness, and the violent removal of the horrid contents from my stomach allowed no pause for intervals. I had been deceived by the very evil I myself had choose to thrive on and at the closing of the chapter of my resistance, I could only witness the smile of the lady once again follow me through the cone of death.

I am now laid to rest without coffin, inside the mud and wet of an open grave. It is raining, vermin crawl across my lifeless body, the stench from the bottle remains to infest the air with its impure redolent, sweeping and floating among the gloom of unfamiliar smoke. The cries and wailings of tortured souls bear witness to the certainty, that I am not alone in my annihilation. In the testing of ghostly vision, I discover that my open grave reaches out for miles like an endless serpent, twisting and slithering, squelching the fruit of life. From the laced confines of my black leather boots, my feet are in a far greater pain than I could ever imagine. They throb, ache and scream, swollen and bleeding from the contamination of trench mud. The bitter knife of arctic breath slices my bones with unmerciful strokes, devouring their core in the jaws of torpid waste. My rifle leans against the mud wall of my mortal tomb, patiently waiting to perform its duty of death. My arms move slowly towards the rifle, it is empty now; the fingers of death are now concealed among the sludge of my discomfort. As the loud whistle screeches its battle scream, life returns to my aching limbs. We rise from the ravine of the damned to tread the doom ground and I, with bayonet soaked in rust and dormant rifle, take my place among those in search of a better death.

There is another whistle sounding through the grey dawn, greater than the first, bellowing and rising in tone. It comes through the mist and champ of forward men, closer and closer, closing in to anxiously embrace its long lost companion. It swallows the earth below my feet, allowing the smoke filled sky to give flight to my helpless soul.

I am with death once again, methylated and white on a softer base, clean and dry in its humility. My legs still solidly throb from the curse of swollen feet, even when they are no longer visible to the human eye. From the chambers of my head I hear the toll of constant bells ringing, ringing, ringing, they will not stop, they will not go away. I am with madness, exchanging the senses of worldly touch for the coarse putrid flesh of distant views. Through my hidden backward thoughts I cringe, only from the absence of reason and to walk the green and yellow pastures of my enchanted home. My being now belongs only to those who will not call my name.

The lady is here, bending over to wash the seeping sanity from my bruised and swollen brow. The bottle returns, I am unable to resist, unable to throw my former arms high in defence as the liquid is again poured down my throat. I swallow the horrid stench that mixes poison into its foulness and leaves me wrenching, twisting, heaving, and violently convulsing in crude torture. She is smiling again, mockingly insulting me with her empty sneer and dispatching me through the tunnel of endless death.

I am now warm although I am only wrapped in thin cotton rags. Extreme heat powders and scorches the land that I now endure. I am a living skeleton framed in my own destitution; my stomach is swollen, bursting with emptiness. All around the parched unfertile ground the wind blows through the crop of hunger, breathing an air of compassion into futile lungs. At the roadside, behind the rocks, within the mud walled huts and on every field and garden, hunger flourishes. There is hunger in the clouds and on the hilltops, hunger among the trees, hunger among the living and hunger among the dead.

The land is baptised in unholy grief, clothed in the garments of ruin and killed by the sword of greed. Babies cling to empty withered breasts and children wail through the bloated eyes of unseen need. I am on my knees allowing the winds to fling dust to paste my blistered lips. I have returned to pain, returned to defend a hopeless cause with prayer and no flesh to cushion the bones of my branch knees. Among the while that equally smudged this forgotten place, I cannot stray nor I cannot run away and if the deepest fog arrived to cover me with its unseen cloak, my soul could never hide. In the absence of reason, I am among the endured spirits of deserted dreams, feeding on the feast of silent promises. I am on the ground now, feasting on the sand of mirage nourishment. My eyes, nose and mouth chocking with raving deceit, begin to smother the chalked earth. I am coughing, spluttering, and punching the ground with decayed fists, begging for strength to remove the weight of my falling weakness. Through the vast heavens of human existence I scream out for food and water, while my heart thumps for the ending of this life.

My body is gently lifted and turned by soft hands; my head now rest on the lap of the lady with the red hair. She is still smiling, smiling, smiling into the few remaining fragments of my reason, while I grasp frantically for the open bottle, thirstily drinking away my pulsating death.

From the corner of an unfamiliar street I stand painless and at ease. There are small oriental people smiling, joking and enjoying the warm sunshine. Children run up and down the street speaking a language in excitement, lost to my recognition. Everywhere it is clean and dry, there is food and adult faces are calm and serious. Ancient trucks and cars slowly pass by, steeping the air with mild irritation. I am at peace within the death that has replaced life yet again. The dogs intelligently juke from the sun's harmful rays; cats scrounge in ally dustbins, mopping their finds with protruding tongues, only to be disturbed by the sport of a passing mouse.

Suddenly without warning there is heat; there is fire, fire reaching up to the clouds and beyond, fire in the streets and at the doorways, fire in the parks and down the alleyways. There are flames, smothering the trucks and cars. People on bicycles and on feet are engulfed with the unexpected mass flock of a terrible inferno. There are screams now, yells of horrendous suffering. Children, adults and animals are smouldering; their burns soaking the mushroomed air with hell's pitiless stench. I am now in accordance with my mortal companions, each of us paying the price for unknown deeds, each of us on bended knees before the dragon of man's fraternal impotence. Each of us lost to fellowship and understanding and in the maze created only for might and power, together we are bewildered. We are now hidden only to ourselves and to those who dwell within the shadows on crumbling walls.

My pain is great, yet no greater than those I fall among. I now only feel for and pity the strangers that I have been born to know so well. Through the dust and angry breeze I call their names, reaching out to grasp tiny fleshless hands, embracing their epitaph with my own charred reflection, whispering unheard requiems to forgotten promises.

Did she truly know when she stole the air from my pulped self, unpainted and raw, that I had embezzled her silence and deprived her red hair and emerald eyes of inflicted sin? In the opening of my lips to swallow yet again the coolness of the liquid death, I consume, enduring the vileness and bitterness with purgatory acceptance. I had no other choice than to face my spiritual fate with the resolve and courage, reserved only for those who stood against impossible odds. The punishment that was handed out to me by some unknown force may have ventured far beyond the borders of its measurement. All that was left to me was to gorge, gulp, and suck the crockery rim like a newborn life yearning to thrive among the throngs of earthly chance.

Did I not have the uncomfortable choice to choose the blackness of my destiny? Was I forced without reckoning to enter the room of my tribulation through the only door available? And as I lay claim to another demise I found that within that short space of confinement, that I had been an island.

I have now arrived at silence within the silence. The grey-washed walls bring forth shadows of black iron bars, reflecting from the moderate light of a harvest moon. Each shadow pointing the direction to doom, like the fingers of a giant skeleton. It is cold and the grey horse hair blanket does no justice to my comfort, nor does the single paper sheet of writing paper sprawled on top of a small wooden table, posing to a black fountain pen. There are no words to scrawl, no friend to bid farewell, no soul to weep for the parting of my will. I am with deep sorrow, crammed full of emptiness inside my solitary room and vacant within my being. I am mourning in a silent dream, sending my conscience to the drums of cobwebbed ears and melting frozen hypocrisy to quench the thirst of dry dehydrated memories.

There is movement, a din slowly slaying the beast of quietness and drawing closer and closer to my man made womb. Falling feet send recognition to the long distant corridor, each moving sole crushes the minutes of earthly smell, each rattle of keys signal the vision of lost and burnt out suns. The time has come; the cell door is flung wildly open. I now hear them speak my name as long white thoughtless faces crowd my body, strapping my trembling hands behind the back of my blood-rushed frame.

Through the open door I am marched, sponge-like and persuaded in straight reluctance. Godly words echo through the dreariness from the saintly lips of a man dressed in black. Each word strong in its mercy, each word yelling for cleanliness among the filth of formal masks. At the wake of the dull barren thud of the second door, I stand solid, offering my neck to the grip of manmade twine. From the mirror of my stupidity I am pleading for light, as the cloak of blacken cloth covers my face from the expression of deserved punishment. The solid base below my feet departs, allowing the descent into apathy and the strangling of my convulsed creation. Each struggle moves me closer to my destination, chocking, gripping, seizing and making worthless the joy of birth.

I am moving, moving towards the rim of the bottle of death, siphoning each drop to flow within the undesired. She is helpful, conscious of my tethered hands, tearing a hole in the cloth with her infant fingernails to offer me each time a glorious and retarded death. Challenging me on every occasion with her sick and demented smile.

For the reward of my transgression, the moments of eternal suffering had been offered to me in drags of poisoned lives. In the confused yet so clear state of my unconsciousness, I nursed the affliction with a heavy repentance. I now accepted my punishment with refined sorrow and deeply regretted the lending of my mind to blighted thoughts. Again the landing of my soul on uncharted ground left me with no cause for surprise.

I am now smothered deep in the core of a wooden hell. My ankles bleed from the fetters of iron clutches, my wrists are swollen and bruised and chains are in abundance in this chapter of death. Unfamiliar tongues once again moan in agony, torture and endured ritual. Their skins are the colour of boiling tar, their eyes and teeth signalling their presence through the vomit and waste of a cursed enclosure.

There is a ray of light from above; chains violently strain in rhythm as the reach out for their portion of worm riddled bread. I am in humiliation beyond my own belief, there is a gross absence of dignity and the departure of human equality is plain to be observed. I dare not cry, I dare not wail to the very heavens, I dare not express weakness in the battlefield of unbleached courage. In the depths of despair with my fellow beings I now seek solace from within the confines of the companionship of suffering.

There is light again, no food dropping from the hatch door, no water or offer of worldly sympathy. We are hurried to the source of light; the strong glare wrenches our eyes with daylight acid as we line up upon the deck of the salt stained heaving ship. There is panic, confusion, sailors are screaming, the ocean is being steeped with breathing bodies weighed down by their heavy chains. I am grasped violently under both arms; the weakness of my body offers poor resistance and the numbness of my shackled legs are dormant in the deep blue waters of prying sharks.

I am drowning; my lungs open to accommodate the rush of salt water, my chest pounds to the hammering of heartbeat's farewell dance. I seek the long red hair and aged face; I look for the haunting green eyes and fixed smile. My death calls her name; her presence bears no vision in mine's present eyes. I am falling deeper and deeper into the cone of departure; I am now lost in my eternal thirst and buried in the tomb of breathless whispers.

I have returned in kind to the flickering of the flaming turf fire. The lady smudges a fireside chair, her scope relevant to my frame sprawled on top of a straw filled mattress. I no longer know my plot in the field of time, darkness or radiant, mortal or spirit. The lady is still dressed with the untouched smile, still holding the sneer of death.

'Are you thirsty Oliver?' she asked
I wanted to say yes, to cry out for moisture, to gulp the pure natural clearness of water.

'No', I replied.

Being only too aware of the horrors that lurked within their clay contents.

'Are you sure Oliver', she said, 'a wee drink might bring some colour back into your pale and getting paler complexion'.

I now stare at the oak table; it is empty save for one solitary crockery bottle standing upright to remove the austere from the surface. I have now become aware of the bottles former contents, for each held a station in time irrelevant to my own; each measure bore no resemblance to my recognition. Their foul matter strayed beyond any sweet-soaked nightmare or dark imagination. These bottles could only contain the beverages that had been mixed in hell.

'You're not very acquiescent Oliver, in fact your manners leave a lot to be desired', she said.

I spoke yet again in weak defiance; I informed her that I had no wish to be confined in her strange abode. I had no desire to be tortured with her mixture of poisons and that these same poisons were the work of dark and dangerous acts. I stopped short of stating that they were probably the ingredients of a soot stained pot and she herself was the proud owner of several nasty black cats.

'You have such a vivid imagination Oliver', she smiled, 'these are medicines mixed and distributed with good and healthy intentions, anyone who has availed of their special formula have already been fully cured'.

I informed her that I had been further from any cure that she might have imagined. I was still quite as ill as I had been on somehow finding myself crossing her door, and broadly speaking, was feeling a lot worse.

'But Oliver', she replied, 'you have not finished the

course, there is still one bottle left and it is important that this bottle also is administered'.

I stared once again at the cream and brown crockery bottle isolated on top of the old bog oak table. I began to question the truth in her words, was this unknown lady flinging her wisdom at the inferiority of my age and condition? Did she seek from within some crude and smoke filled vision to possess the very crust of my already tainted soul? Or did she in all truth, seek through some hidden meaning that dwelled behind her soft green eyes, to free me from my rising pain and worry? For this lady who had been fashioned from some distant mould in time, had possessed sight unaffordable to normal vision. This lady, who prodded my injured soul with mythical twigs, could reach deep into the depths of my mind and body and understood what grew within.

Did I have the will to inhabit yet again the contents of the last bottle? Perhaps I would forever roam in places far from the imagination. Perhaps this final push over the edge of my suffering would deliver me deep down into the volcano of annulled awareness. Whatever decision I choose to make, that same lady who awaited the echo from my lips, already knew what would sound from the drums of my vocal chords.

'You have made the right decision Oliver', she said, 'this bottle is without question the icing on the cake'.

I now watched her childlike movements as she playfully made her way to the table. The bottle appeared in her hand and as quickly as my mind and eyes could focus, it was lunged at my unopened mouth with all the violence of a spear on its sordid path of murder.

The dam of my throat now falls before the deluge of drowned resistance. The bottle's contents flows through the sweetness of its own flavour to gently stream once again. Its smoothness far from the mixture of the others was so familiar, yet it held no likeness to the present portrait. I cried out for more of its heavenly aroma, I yearned from far inside my youthful spirit ,for it to gush abundantly and for all eternity. I screamed with solid and rightful joy as I made my way through the door that would lead me to a beautiful and reverend death.

7

A LIGHT THROUGH THE NIGHT

I was cold yet the fire that flowed through my life-scorched veins contented me and offered comfort to the knowledge of the night. I am alone again, sheltered by ruined stone walls peppered by green moss. The moon's giant lantern gives vision equal to day and whilst I strain my ears for worldly tones, I strive to hear the distant bark of an absent dog. I hear it call out in unique canine brogue, unmoved and then approaching. I hear it again unmoved and then closer, louder, entering the confines of my stone memorial where I lie composed and scarred.

There are many moons now, glaring the night air with ringed relief. I see faces; faces that I once loved and still do. Expressions that were once cold but are now warm by the discovery of my feeble frame perched on top of untouched ground. The dark uniform of fear now holds no menace as he kneels beside me in gold relief; his police badge reflecting the many lights like a cascade of newly discovered diamonds. I know his face; I know the familiar eyes and deep crevices of the school inspector. I see my mother on her knees beside me now, glorifying God in her own pure way, shaking the very pearl gates with the echo of her thanksgiving. I see James standing by one of the walls, his toothless smile offering no bitterness for the slaughtering of his trust. Perched on top of a lonely stone there is Peter. His folded down waders smudged with mud and grass, inflicted not by his pursuit of me for some wrong doing, but concern for my welfare. At the opening of the walls, Sonny's blessed face soaked in sweat and tears soars in its platinum presence. And there was Shep the founder of my discovery, waging his tail in broad contentment. There were more; shopkeepers, farmers, skivers and loathers of non-alcoholic beverages. Hundreds lit the pathway in which I was carried, free and untouched by any revenge or malice.

I have returned to the solid shadow of my former being, my heart could no longer beat with hate or malignant contempt, my brain could no longer hatch dark-filled thoughts. I had indeed finished the lady's crockery course and with all due fairness and honesty, her cure now came upon me like a clean unblighted potato dug from a famine field. Her promise had wooed my trust and her sneer was now translated to a smile, a smile that I etched on the bark of a tree that now grew in the garden of my soul.

At the side of my hospital bed the story surrounding my escapade began to unfold chapter by chapter, each word flung in person from the lips of my many visitors. The cheerful Sonny prided himself in once again being reinstated as supreme baker of currant scones. The search party that tramped the fields and marshy bogs in pursuit of my whereabouts decided that stomach tanks had to be refuelled whatever the grade. Shep had arrived on his doorstep with a litter of handsomely marked miniature Sheepdogs, and removed the heavy chains of suspicion from around his narrow neck. My mother never left my bedside, informing me that due to circumstances that my youthful mind could not yet fathom I would not be punished. The school inspector who was also a part time policeman had feared for his life and on realizing the barrel of a gun, reacted in a way that was natural to those in troubled times. James' air rifle had been returned after violence was offered in exchange for its absence. A visit to the dentist's dungeon of tortured nerves had removed Angelica's heavenly presence for an hour, and plunging the classroom into a sea of wretchedness. When she returned and had been informed by the headmaster that my visit to the school that morning had been swift, troublesome and fully expected of my temperament. Angelica had departed troubled, and made calls to my home and several people who might know my whereabouts. Word soon spread about the attempted assault on the school inspector, and without calling on the services of a mathematician, two and two were quickly added together.

As I lay in the hospital bed until the eve of the festive day allowed me to take my thankful leave, and the wound caused by the scraping of my ribs by the bullet from a small calibre pistol had healed, I was visited every day by the school inspector. Among all the topics that reaped our minds for fodder in which we could converse, was why did I attack him and not the head master? Did I really believe that an air rifle could do any harm from the distance that I was positioned? And how on earth did I manage to get my hands on a First World War bullet in prestige condition? I informed him of my naivety of all accounts, especially the nine points of the law. I assured him with all sincerity that never again would I grasp in my small hand any item however ineffective that would threaten the meaning of life.

As the school inspector departed offering a scratch of wonder to his lightly clad head, I could only stare in confused awareness at the brown and cream coloured crockery bottle at ease on top of my bedside locker. Free from any liquid it contained a metal fountain pen, a link of rusted iron chain, a fragment of ivory and a child's charred handkerchief. I asked myself this question, within these mythical items of stone reality, would the school inspector have really found his answer?

The End